એક નવો દિવસ
Ek Navo Divas
A New Day

Reader's guide

Each page has three sentences about the fun filled day
Reyan is having with his parents.

For rhyming effect, read the Gujarati sentences on each spread together.

First line - A Gujarati sentence in Gujarati script.
Second line - English transliteration* for the Gujarati sentence.
Third line - English translation of the Gujarati sentence.

* Special alphabet in the English transliteration for the Gujarati sentence

- ā - ch(aa)r or chār - represents long a, or 'aa' sound
- ä - ty(ān) or tyä / ü - sh(un) or shü - represent ending nasal sounds
- ṇ - mākhaṇ / ḷ - maḷshe - represent retroflex alphabet

નમસ્તે મમ્મી! જુઓ, સૂરજ-દાદા આવ્યા !
Namaste mummy! Juo suraj-dādā āvyā !
Hello Mom! Look, the sun is out!

સવારના નાસ્તામાં મને આજે શું મળશે ?
Savārnā nāstāmā mane āje shü maḷshe ?
What will I get for breakfast today?

તને ગરમ આલુ પરાઠા પર માખણ મળશે.
Tane garam āloo parāthā par mākhaṇ maḷshe.
You will get a hot potato flatbread with butter.

આજે ચાલો બહાર જઈ કંઈક મજા કરીશું !
Aaje chālo bahār jai kaink majā karishü !
Let's go outside and do something fun today!

ફટાફટ કપડાં બદલી, જોડાં પહેરીશું.

Phatāphat kapadā badli, jodā paherishū.

Let's quickly change our clothes and wear our shoes.

રેયાન, બારીની બહાર તને શું શું દેખાય છે ?
Reyan, bārini bahār tane shū shū dekhāy chhe ?
Reyan, what do you see outside the window?

એક ગાડી, બે બસ, ત્રણ ટ્રક, ચાર ઝાડ ને પાંચ પંખી દેખાય છે.
Ek gādi, be bus, traṇ truck, chār jhād ne pānch pankhi dekhāy chhe.
I see one car, two buses, three trucks, four trees and five birds.

ચાલો ચાલો, સફરજનથી ભરેલાં ઝાડ શોધીએ .
Chālo chālo, sapharjan thi bharelā jhād shodhie .
Let's go, search for some trees full of apples.

લાલ લાલ તોડીએ, ને લીલા લીલા છોડીએ .

Lāl lāl todie, ne leelā leelā chhodie .

Pluck the red apples, leave the green ones.

આજે જમવા માટે છે ઈડલી-વડા-સાંબાર.
Aaje jamvā māte chhe idli-vadā-sāmbār.
Today, lunch is rice cakes and lentil fritters with lentil curry.

એક એક કરીને ખાવાથી સ્વાદ મળે મજેદાર.

Ek ek karine khāvāthi swād maḷe majedār.

Eating them one by one makes them taste even better.

જુઓ! ગાયો અને ઘોડા બેઠાં છે નજીક અહીંયાં .
Juo! Gāyo ane ghodā bethā chhe najeek ahinyä
Look! Horses and cows are sitting over here.

ચાલો ચાલો, તેમને ગાજર ખવડાવીએ જઈ ત્યાં.
Chālo chālo, temne gājar khavdāvie jaee tyä.
Let's go feed them carrots over there.

વાહ! જુઓ લાલ, કેસરી, પીળાં, લીલાં, નીલાં ને જાંબુડી ફૂલોની શાન.

Vāh! Juo lāl, kesari, peeḷä, leelä, neelä ne jāmbudi phuloni shān.

Wow! Look at the beautiful red, orange, yellow, green, blue, and purple flowers

ત્યાં દૂર આકાશમાં જો, સતરંગી છે ઇન્દ્રધનુની કમાન .

Tyä dur ākāshmā jo, satarangee chhe indradhanuni kamān .

The sky has an arc of a rainbow full of seven colors over there.

ગરમીમાં તો ઠંડી ઠંડી કુલ્ફી મને બહુ ભાવે !
Garmimä to thandi thandi kulfi mane bahu bhāve !
During summer, cold cold ice cream feels good!

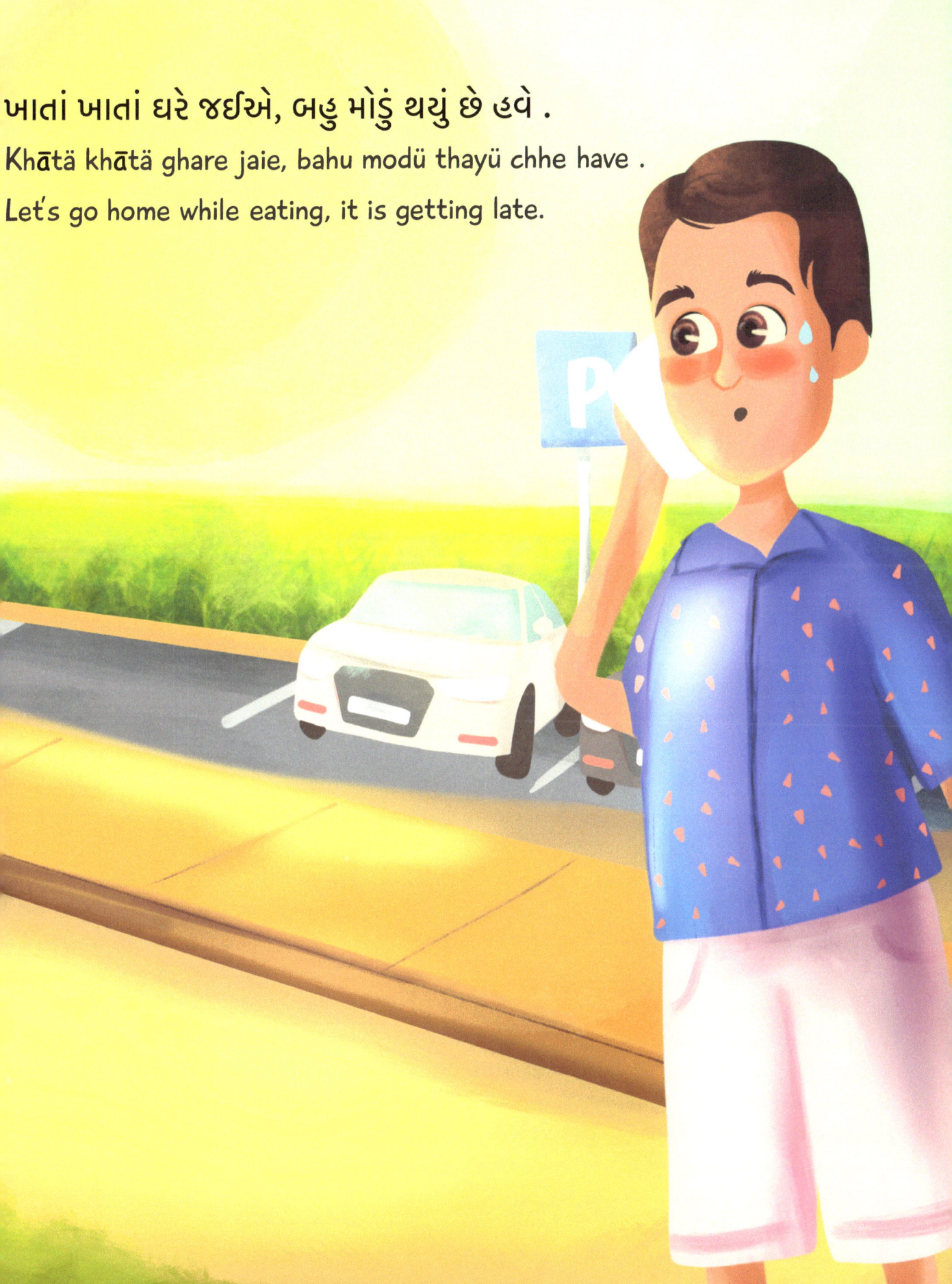

ખાતાં ખાતાં ઘરે જઈએ, બહુ મોડું થયું છે હવે.
Khātā khātā ghare jaie, bahu modū thayū chhe have.
Let's go home while eating, it is getting late.

ચાલો હવે નાહી ધોઈને સાફ થઈ જઈએ.
Chālo have nāhi dhoine sāph thai jaie.
Let's go, take a bath now to get clean.

રાતના જમવામાં છે સરસ રાજમા-ભાતની જોડી .
Rātnā jamvāmā chhe saras rājmā-bhātni jodi .
Dinner is a yummy combo of kidney beans & rice

જમી કરીને પછી મને શું મળશે ખીર થોડી ?

Jami karine pachhi mane shü maḷshe kheer thodi ?

After finishing dinner, can I get a little rice pudding?

રમકડાં કરતાંયે વધારે, ચોપડીઓ મને પ્યારી .

Ramakadā kartāye vadhāre, chopadio mane pyāri .

More than toys, I love my books.

છેલ્લી ચોપડી વાંચો, પછી કરો સૂવાની તૈયારી.

Chhelli chopadi vāncho, pachhi karo suvāni taiyāri.

This is the last book, after this get ready for bed.

ઝગમગતા તારા અને ચાંદને લઈ અંધારી રાત છે આવી .
Jhagmagtā tārā ane chāndne lai andhāri raat che āvi .
The sparkling stars and moon are out with the dark night.

ગુજરાતી-અંગ્રેજી શબ્દકોશ અને રમત
Gujarati-Angreji Shabdkosh Ane Ramat
Gujarati-English Glossary and Games

શું તમે ઇન્દ્રધનુમાં રંગ ભરીને, નીચે લખેલા બધા રંગોનાં નામ કહી શકો ?
Shü tame indradhanumā rang bharine, niche lakhelā badhā rangonā nām kahi shako ?
Can you color the rainbow and name all the colors listed below?

રંગ	Rang	Colors
લાલ	Lāl	Red
કેસરી/નારંગી	Kesari/Nārangi	Orange
પીળો	Peeḷo	Yellow
લીલો	Leelo	Green
નીલો	Neelo	Blue
જાંબુડી	Jāmbudee	Purple
કાળો	Kāḷo	Black
સફેદ	Saphed	White

શું તમે નીચે આપેલાં ઘડિયાળોમાં બધા અંકો વાંચી શકો છો?
Shü tame niche āpelā ghadiyāḷomā badhā anko vānchi shako chho?
Can you read all the numbers written in the clocks below?

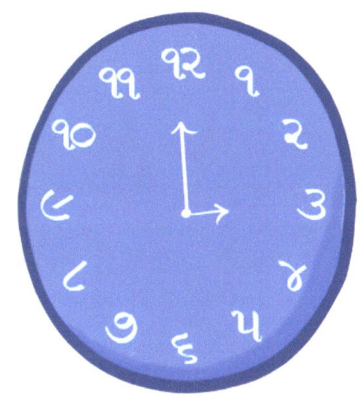

અંકો/સંખ્યા		Anko/Sankhya	Numbers	
૧	એક	Ek	1	One
૨	બે	Be	2	Two
૩	ત્રણ	Traṇ	3	Three
૪	ચાર	Chār	4	Four
૫	પાંચ	Pānch	5	Five
૬	છ	Chha	6	Six
૭	સાત	Sāt	7	Seven
૮	આઠ	Aath	8	Eight
૯	નવ	Nav	9	Nine
૧૦	દસ	Dus	10	Ten
૧૧	અગિયાર	Agiyār	11	Eleven
૧૨	બાર	Bār	12	Twelve

શું તમે વાર્તા વાંચતી વખતે આ વિરોધી શબ્દોની જોડીઓ પર ધ્યાન આપ્યું?
Shü tame vārtā vānchti vakhte aa virodhi shabdoni jodeeo par dhyān āpyü?
Did you notice these pairs of opposites while reading the book?

દિવસ - Divas - Day   રાત - Raat - Night

સૂરજ - Suraj - Sun   ચાંદ - Chānd - Moon

ગરમી - Garmi - Hot   ઠંડી - Thandi - Cold

ફટાફટ - Phatāphat - Quickly   મોડું - Modü - Late

હવે - Have - Now   પછી - Pachhi - Later

નજીક - Najeek - Near   દૂર - Dur - Far

અહીંયાં - Ahinyä - Here   ત્યાં - Tyä - There

થોડી - Thodi - Little   વધારે - Vadhāre - More

About the Author

Anuja Mohla, DO is a physician turned author with her award winning debut book "Ek Naya Din." Born and raised in New Delhi (India), Anuja immigrated to America as a teenager. She found her passion for writing through her desire to empower her son to be multilingual. Anuja realized the challenge her generation faces in teaching children about their heritage. She founded 'Apni heritage' with the goal of creating multilingual products that will help young parents, like her, teach their native language to the next generation. In her spare time, she loves to cook, and build on her love for Bollywood via movies, music, and dance. For more information about her company, Apni Heritage, please check www.apniheritage.com.

About the Illustrator

Noor Alshalabi is a Jordan-based illustrator who started drawing ever since she learnt how to hold a pencil. After getting her BA in Visual Arts and Design, she pursued her dream of turning her imagination into reality through children's books. You can always find her with a cup of coffee, curled up with a good book, watching movies, playing with her pet bird, spending time with a friend, or going for a hike. Nature is both her source of inspiration and relaxation.

About the Translator

Priti Gosar-Patil is an IT professional, Bharatanatyam artiste and linguaphile who has taught Marathi, Gujarati and Sanskrit languages to children, adults and fellow artists, beginning from her children - Uday, Vibha and husband - Deepak. She has translated books from Marathi and Gujarati to English, and many storyweaver children's books to Gujarati & Marathi languages. Priti aspires to enable enthusiastic parents and grandparents to teach their language and dialect to future generations. She wishes to strengthen their roots so they can fly far and wide, and be able to come back to their own culture through their language.

Printed in the USA
CPSIA information can be obtained
at www.ICGtesting.com
LVHW071627131123
763828LV00014B/47